Life, Orange to Pear

JOHN BRANTINGHAM

BAMBOO
DART
PRESS

LOS ANGELES † NEW YORK † LONDON † SYDNEY

Life, Orange to Pear by John Brantingham

ISBN: 978-1-947240-07-0

eISBN: 978-1-947240-08-7

Some of these stories have been published in the following magazines, collections, and museums: The Sasse Museum, *Shark Reef Magazine*, *(mac)ro(mic)*, and Ad Hoc Fiction's *Flash Fiction Anthology*.

For information:

Bamboo Dart Press

chapbooks@bamboodartpress.com

Curated and operated by Dennis Callaci and Mark Givens

Bamboo Dart Press 002

www.pelekinesis.com

www.bamboodartpress.com

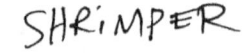
www.shrimperrecords.com

Contents

For Annie

Orange

You're sitting on the back porch, peeling an orange, getting down to the deeply spiritual part of the orange down where you can taste the bitter rind just from smelling it because you're pulling off the skin, high, close to your nose.

This is the way you did it when you were a kid and you needed a minute away from life because you were dealing with the deep and existential questions of childhood, questions that dealt with monsters and homework and your dad and whether or not you were going to be able to make it through to adulthood.

On the angry days when your mind spun all the worst possibilities, you'd take an orange from the tree in the backyard, and you could lose yourself inside it, and on this day when you have found out that your presence will not be required at work tomorrow or any time after that, despite the fact that you have a four year old and a wife who is underpaid, you find yourself trying to lose yourself into this childhood orange and not making it, you suppose because your face is streaming with the tears of terror and incompetence.

That's when you notice Cyndi, standing at the back door in her little overalls. She's watching you and sucking on the first three fingers of her right hand, trying to understand what's happening.

You stare back a moment, and you could say anything, but your mouth lands on, "You wanna see a trick, Gumdrop?" You hold out your hand to her, and she comes over close enough that you can grab her and put her on your lap. "This is how you make everything better, okay?"

"Okay."

You start to peel the orange again and say, "Breathe in, okay?"

"Okay."

"Isn't that good?"

"Yeah."

"This is your trick for knowing that everything in the world is good." Cyndi doesn't say anything to this, but she leans back hard against your chest, and you can feel her breathing deep, going into that spiritual world of the orange. You can see into her mind because it was the same mind you had at her age, and it's true. Everything in this world is good.

Nature Redone

There is some comfort, you suppose that after you die, nature will repurpose your body, insects feasting on your blood, dandelions growing out of your flesh, or so you think as you watch little Cyndi resting up against the carved tree trunk in the park outside the library. When the tree died, they called in an artist who turned it into a thing of beauty as maybe your corpse will be too in those days after you pass.

This morning Cyndi asked you if everyone goes to heaven after they die, and you told her no, because that's what you believe. Your wife knew that she wasn't marrying a Catholic, and if she wants to fill Cyndi with religion, she may, but that's not who you are.

Cyndi asked if you thought your soul lived on, and you said that no, you thought it was a full stop, which is a hell of a thing to say to a child, but you promised never to lie, and you keep that promise, more or less.

And Cyndi went into a private inner room of her mind and found a rabbit puppet that she's been wearing on her hand ever since. The rabbit talks to her, and she talks back. Sometimes they tell each other true things and sometimes they just gossip.

Here in this park where you took Cyndi this afternoon to derail your wife's narrative that you are a cruel father sometimes, the rabbit whispers something into Cyndi's ear.

Cyndi says, no it's full stop, the end, no more.

The rabbit whispers something else.

Cyndi shakes her head sadly. No, she says, it's not about fairness.

Come on, you say, breaking up her morality play, and maybe this is an act of cruelty too. After all, perhaps this is just her way of processing and choosing your wife's religion or your philosophy or some other thing that is neither.

You scoop her up in your arms and lift her above your head and say touch it. She reaches as far as she can and puts her hand on the back of a bee carved out of this tree that has become a vanitas.

What does it feel like? you ask.

It's cool, she says.

Does it hurt? you ask.

No? but there is a quaver in her voice.

Does it feel all right?

Yes?

You lower her and hug her. This tree is dead, you say. But that is all right. It's beautiful too. That's what I believe.

And she tears up a little so you hold her close and think that what you said is very close to the truth, as close as words can get but there is something else in what you believe, but it hides from you. It is something about faith. It is something about hope.

You feel a softness at your ear, and you realize that it's the rabbit that has never spoken to anyone but Cyndi ever before.

She speaks now through Cyndi's whisper. But you don't know, do you?

No, you say.

No one really knows, do they?

No.

And you can feel her crying, and she puts her head against your chest. You promised her that you would never lie to her, and you've kept that promise as well as you could, so you let yourself cry your quiet tears now too.

Go Back to Sleep

Cyndi's silence startles you. She's sitting next to you at the picnic table, her legs not swinging, but rigidly pointing down, her face wrinkled into a worried wisdom as she stares into the forest. "What is it, honey?" your wife asks her, and she lifts a finger pointing the direction she's facing like a little kid would in one of those horror movies you watched in the 80s, this being the moment that the peace of the perfect family is first ruined. You have no idea what she's pointing at so you ask, "What?"

"The cat," she whines, and you and your wife both turn, and you don't see anything, but your wife says, "Oh my God," and grabs your child and heads to the van leaving you out there alone.

When you get into the van, you say, "What, what, what?" and your wife points the way your daughter did, and now you have two possessed family members, the plot in your film growing, you becoming the hero who is tasked to save them all. You say, "I just don't see. . ." but then you do see a mountain lion watching you.

That night, back in camp, Cyndi asks, "Do you think Josephine will creep into our tent tonight?" making you regret that you taught her the word "creep" last Halloween. At breakfast, she says, "I think Josephine is watching us."

"Where is she?"

Cyndi's eyes go as wide as that girl's in *Poltergeist,* which you now completely regret watching when you were twelve. She says,

"Everywhere."

On the hike, Cyndi holds her breath and says, "Josephine is hungry like the wolf." And you wish to god you'd smashed all those Duran Duran cds once the 20th century ran itself out.

You ask, "Why do you call her Josephine?"

Cyndi shakes her head seriously. "No, that's what Krampus calls her," and you feel your wife's eyes on you, knowing that she's going to make you swear to stop telling the kid scary stories.

That night, you awaken out of a dead sleep into the moonlit room that your family tent has become to find Cyndi staring at you, those wide eyes again. "Why does Josephine want to eat us?" It's a serious question, pulling you out of whatever comfortable dream you had just been occupying.

"Go back to sleep," you say, but her little hand is pressing against your stomach, so you hold her. "She doesn't want to eat you. She's watching over you to make sure that you're safe." You kiss your child on the cheek, let her snuggle in your sleeping bag with you.

And as Cyndi slips back into her dream world, you realize that she has passed her curse on to you, your eyes widening, your mind telling you that Josephine is circling, that Josephine is there, that Josephine has taken residence in a little spot in your brain. The movie has flipped, a private horror show just for you.

Weirdo

You wake Christmas morning to find your daughter Cyndi, kneeling next to you in bed, her little hand on your chin, her eyes watching your eyes. "I think Santa Claus," she says, "might be a weirdo."

You turn to look at your wife, but she's still passed out hard, so you scoop Cyndi into your arms and walk her down the hall toward the tree. "Why do you say that?" you ask, thinking that it's too early for this kind of drama, but if there is to be drama, you might just want to lean into it. Maybe seven years old is old enough to know the truth about Santa Claus. Merry fucking Christmas, kid.

Cyndi looks deeply into your eyes. "He left some weird shit in my stocking," she says.

And you think that it's too early to figure out where she learned to talk like that. Also, maybe that should be something her mother does unless she learned it from you. You don't answer, but instead come over to the fireplace where Cyndi dumped her stocking out, and now lying on the carpet is a Jesus candle, top ramen, a Billy Joel cd, and about thirty brazil nuts. You and the wife were pretty blasted last night, but you can remember doing this vaguely and thinking it was funny for some reason. Your wife laughed too.

You sit cross-legged in front of the pile and try to rub some life into your face. Cyndi places a hand on your leg and says, "I mean, what is all this shit?"

You take a deep breath. "Beats the shit out of me. Maybe Santa is a weirdo."

She's staring suspiciously at the presents under the tree, and you scan your memory, trying to reference wrapping something late at night. Nothing comes to mind, although there is a long package you don't recognize.

"I just don't know what's going on in this world," she says. "It's like God is dead."

You nod at the insight. Maybe God is dead for your little girl. "Maybe Krampus got into the house instead of Santa."

Cyndi looks at the chimney, crawls over and looks up it. "Do we have a gun?"

"Not likely."

"Then, you're going to have to stand watch with your baseball bat waiting for him to come back."

"I don't have a baseball bat."

Cyndi smiles at you. She goes over to the gifts under the tree and brings the present you didn't recognize. She hands it to you. "Merry Christmas, Daddy," she says. "Mommy and I picked it out."

You unwrap it to find that they have given you a bat signed by Goose Gossage, who was a man you admired for his name rather than his game. Hell of a pitcher, but who would want his bat? Anyway, you were always a Dodger fan, but somehow your wife and daughter always think you love him. The bat and Cyndi's smile makes you want to cry, makes you want to stop drinking. You know you're not going to, but at this moment, you really want to.

She puts her head on your chest. "If Santa or Krampus or anyone else comes down that chimney, you beat him until he's dead, okay Daddy?"

You hug your precious little psycho and say, "Don't worry about a thing pumpkin patch. I won't let any weirdo into this house ever again."

Tooth Fairy

You wake to Cyndi pulling your eyelids apart, the sky just beginning to lighten, your wife still asleep. "Are you awake?"

Normally you'd tell her to go back to bed, but she's wearing such solemnity, you say, "Yeah, what's going on?"

"I think the tooth fairy is crap."

You sit up hoping this will stir your wife. Either she's not awake or she's faking, but you're on your own. "Why don't you believe?"

"Oh, I believe. I just think he's a jerk. I put a tooth under my pillow four days ago, and nothing happened."

"You lost a tooth?" She pulls back her cheek to show you. "Why didn't you tell me?"

"It's kind of creepy that he sneaks into houses looking for body parts. I didn't want you to freak."

"Well, thank you."

"I've been up nights thinking about all of it."

"All of what?"

"The tooth fairy, God, Santa Claus. I think I'm done with all of them."

You're sure your wife's breathing has changed. If she wasn't faking before, she is now. "I thought you wanted to go to church."

"Not anymore. I'm concerned about their motives."

You nod at this, one of the great questions she will be faced with. "Sure," you say.

"What do they want with us? I just don't get it."

"Neither do I," you say, and you're not being glib. You've wrestled with this your whole life.

"Maybe we should be content to be among people."

"That's a sound conclusion." You pull her between you and your wife, put her under the covers. In a moment, she's sleeping, and you wish you could slip a dollar under her pillow, but that would shake the intellectual framework she's devised over the last few nights. You and your wife are going to have to talk about what you're supposed to tell a kid, not that you haven't before. For now, however, you're happy to watch the light on the ceiling shift and wonder what it is that you believe. You wonder if you've ever believed anything at all.

Avocado

You try to steer Cyndi in her Hulk costume away from the house three doors down where the pediatrician lives. He opens the door and pulls an avocado and a toothbrush out of a basket and tosses them into her pillowcase. He says, "Happy Halloween."

Cyndi thanks him, but you can't help yourself. You say, "You know it takes a special kind of asshole to give a child a lecture instead of a piece of candy." You point into his basket overflowing with the Earth's bounty. "Is that a beet?"

He cocks his head. "What? Did you have a couple of drinks before you took your kid out trick or treating?"

Of course, you did, but only because you forgot it was Halloween, and anyway, you thought you'd mouthwashed the smell away. Apparently not. "Yes, madam," you say, "but tomorrow, I'll wake up sober, and you'll still be a shithead." The quotation is right on the top of your head because you've been teaching Churchill in your graduate seminar for the last two weeks. You know you got it wrong and the "madam" probably confused the guy a little, but it feels like a good retort, so you spin on your back heel and catch up with Cyndi who's sitting on the front lawn.

By now, the guy's slammed his door, so you say to her, "If you want, we can throw the produce through that fucker's front window."

"No, Dad, no. I'm the peaceful Hulk." This is probably why she drew a Mercedes Benz symbol on the chest of her costume. She brings the avocado up to her nose and inhales and smiles and then lifts it up to you.

You take it and breathe it in, and it fills you up. "You make a good point, Gumdrop, and besides there's more loot to be taken on this street."

She takes it back and smells it once more. "It's so good," she says. "It's just so fucking good."

Rattlesnake and Rabbit

Cyndi comes home from camp completely obsessed with rabbits. She saw a little one eaten by a rattlesnake early in the morning when she slipped away at dawn to hike alone through the desert.

You ask, You went off by yourself?

She is a serious eight year old, with the eyes of a forty-three year old woman who has seen war or plague or faminine, something like that.

I just needed to get away, she says. Those girls can be a lot.

You can't disagree with her there, and since she's been home, she's been researching rabbits, reading about them in encyclopedias, begging you to go out to the scrub and help her find them. It's been three days that she's been back, and you've been hoping that her attention will snap to something else, but it hasn't yet, and you think it might not for a while.

She begs you to get a book about rabbits. So you take her to the bookstore, holding her hand as you walk the aisle. The salesperson takes you to the children's section and finds books about cute bunnies.

Still holding your hand, she looks up to you and says, These are books for little kids. She looks at the salesperson and says, I want to learn about death.

The woman looks at you, but you deadeye her back. You ask, You have any books like that?

The best that she can do is a field guide of North American mammals, which you bring home, and Cyndi reads religiously for a couple of days.

Eventually, you bring it up. How goes the reading? you ask.

She shrugs. It only gives me facts.

What do you want?

More, she says. Can we go find some rabbits?

So you do. You take her out to the desert, and since you live out in California, the desert isn't far. You drive down a dirt road where you're sure that you've seen them, and when you park in the early morning light, it doesn't take you long to find them. Cyndi's fallen asleep, so you scoop her up in your arms and wake her. You point out at some bushes and say, There they are.

She leans forward and tenses and watches them flitting in bushes and then pausing, then moving again. She watches them for a while and groans her way back into a resting position in your arms.

What's wrong? you ask. I thought you wanted to see rabbits. There they are.

I know, she says. Thank you.

So what's wrong?

I'm trying to understand if they're fulfilling their destiny by becoming food.

You look down at her. What? Where did you learn . . . But you don't finish the question. You know where she learned to talk like that. Well, you say, that would be your mother's argument of course. Do you think she's right?

I don't know. Do you?

I don't know, you say. Then you think better of it. No, I don't.

She doesn't say anything, but she asks you a question with her eyes.

I think that the world is often chaotic, and sometimes things just die. I also think that the snake was able to live.

She nods and puts a couple of fingers in her mouth. She's not satisfied with the answer, but that's all right by you. It's not a satisfying answer.

She pulls her fingers out. Do you think there are snakes out there? She points at the bushes near the rabbits.

Yes.

Do you think they'll eat some of those rabbits?

Yes.

Okay, she says.

You watch them for a little while until you can feel her falling back to sleep in her arms. It's still early, and that's a big concept for a child, so you put her in the car. She is, you realize, more like you than her mother, and that's too bad. Maybe Cyndi will have the good sense to grow up to be a composite of the two of you. Maybe she will be something else. Maybe she will be a philosopher. Maybe she's just starting the big push through life that everyone does, and she has a lifetime of unanswerable questions ahead of her.

All of this is unknowable so you watch the rabbits scratching out their lives as best they can as she sleeps in the car.

Useless Bastard

You listen to Cyndi unzip her sleeping bag, shuffle out of it, unzip her tent, and pad her way across the campground, and you wonder if it was too much for her to have her own tent this year, if you should have told her no to that one, and you'll talk to the wife about that later maybe, but for now she's found the part of the tent closest to your head, and she whispers, "Dad?"

"Do you think that stupid fucking boy is around here?" There's fear rising in her voice, the same fear that you used to hear when she obsessed about Krampus, but this is different, you know.

"You shouldn't call people stupid," you say.

"When we were around the campfire with all those people, he said I have a nice ass. He kept staring at me too."

Cyndi is twelve. "You can call that useless fucking bastard stupid all you want." You try to remember if you would have said that to a girl when you were their age. You don't think so, but if you did, you would have been a useless fucking bastard. Stupid too.

"Do you think he's around?"

You slip out of the tent conscious that your wife is awake and listening to this, testing to see if you're going to say and do the right thing, and she's right to do it, but you're formulating a plan of action, and not coming up with anything that seems useful or good.

Outside, the moon is down and the stars are up. You watch for satellites, but it's too late for them now. Cyndi is hugging herself. You say, "Yeah, he probably is around, sleeping in one of those tents." You nod off to where you think his family is staying.

"I hate that guy. I can't sleep."

There is probably something you could say here that is wise and wonderful, but given your track record, you know that you're more likely to make a stupid joke that makes everything just a little bit worse, so you say instead, "What would you like to do?" It's not maybe something Addicus Finch would have come up with, but at least you're not making things worse. Maybe. You're giving Cyndi a little power. Maybe. You're acknowledging her needs and making her feel safer. Maybe.

"I don't know. I can't sleep."

"Let's build a little fire then," you say and you do, Cyndi pulling her sleeping bag, the one with the cartoon images of the Muppet Babies, out of her tent and sits next to you, pushing herself against you for warmth. You've got your little flask of bourbon, and you take a sip.

"You're going to drink?" she asks.

You shrug. "It keeps you warm." She eyes it as you take a little sip. "You want a taste?"

She cocks her head a little, and the thought of that useless, stupid fucking bastard is gone at least for this moment from her head. Maybe. The fire has built itself up to a little yellow dancer and her cheeks flick with it.

She takes the flask out of your hand and sniffs, making a face. You think after the scent, she's not going to want anything, but in this, like so much in life, you are wrong, and she takes a mouth full, frowning, but swallowing it down. "That's awful," she says.

"Yeah, it's not great."

"I am never going to drink again."

"Good."

"Do you think he's over there?"

"Yes, I do," you say. "But I'm here too."

And you put your arm around her and feel her body untense by degrees. You feel her falling asleep against you, and you're pretty sure this is the last time she's going to trust you like this, heading into her teenage years as she is. It's good to feel her going to sleep, but you're pretty sure that you're not going to be able to, not for thinking about, talking to the useless bastard's parents tomorrow. You rehearse what it is you're going to say. You dream of the things that you wish you could do to him.

The School of Art and Enterprises

You're leaning up against your car, waiting when your daughter Cyndi comes out the front door of the school painted in a kind of swirling dance of colors, and Cyndi's talking to a boy, her hand on his shoulder, the kind of boy who broods a little too much and looks at his feet and then up through his bangs at her to show that he has wisdom beyond his thirteen years, and Cyndi brushes it back, and that's when the earthquake starts to shake this world of dancing color and children who are birthing themselves into adulthood, and you're a real Californian, so earthquakes have never scared you, but you flash a smidge of guilt because you're a father too, and things like that are supposed to scare you, except Cyndi's a real Californian too, and she laughs at the world going akimbo and grabs onto this boy and twirls herself into his arms, and they dance into each other trying to find their legs among these kids who are dancing just to stay upright, in front of this painting that is dancing to show that this is a place for kids like her, and you're remembering your first dances with Cyndi's mother, the dances that stay with you all your life, and Cyndi's having one of those dances right now, and it's not scary in any way except in the way that the mysteries of love are terrifying and joyful all at once.

Basic Dignity

You press your hand against the door as if you're checking for fire and say, "Cyndi, it's going to be all right."

You can hear her sobbing, but she manages to say, "I can't marry a man who doesn't understand that basic dignity demands that agnostics respect other people's personal religious beliefs."

"Well honey, maybe you don't have to have everything figured out at the age of fourteen."

Something catches in her throat. There's silence before she opens the door. "Maybe you're right, Dad."

"And maybe take a break from dating."

"Maybe I'll become a lesbian."

"I don't think that's a choice you get to make, but if you are, good on you."

She hugs you. "Life seems to be a minefield of existential crises."

"And it doesn't get any easier," you say. You don't tell her that it only gets harder. Let that part be a surprise.

Stump

You're over at Drew's house with Cyndi and your wife, during one of his I-might-just-be-the-wealthiest-man-in-town parties complete with a string quartet and catering staff and the most expensive booze you've ever seen which is why you've had your share and Cyndi's too because what the hell, she's too young to drink. You're about to head for the bar to get started on your wife's share when you notice Cyndi, glaring at Drew's coffee table.

"What's up?" you ask her.

"Can you believe this?"

"The table?"

"Yeah, look at it." The middle section of a giant tree that someone put legs on and shellacked until it was smooth like marble.

"It's a table made from a tree cookie," you say.

"Yeah, a sequoia tree cookie." You cock your head at it. It's a big table, but it's not sequoia sized. It's not even redwood sized. Cyndi's at that age when everything is an injustice that she must rail against, and you like that about her. She's a good person and all of that, but on the other hand, she's also kind of wearing you out with cause after cause.

On the other hand, you know that Drew's always had kind of a thing for your wife, so you say, "Son-of-a-bitch, you're right."

"I don't believe it. I thought these trees were protected."

"Go grab your mother. We're leaving in protest."

Cyndi heads off looking for your wife while you slip over to grab one more drink. Drew comes up behind you and grabs you by the arm. "I wanted to show you something," he says. He takes you into his study, which has been locked all afternoon, closes the door behind him, locks it.

"What's going on?"

"I just bought something at auction the other day, that I think you'd get but maybe not everyone else would. You know about the Boer War, right?"

"I wrote my dissertation on it. I teach a couple of seminars."

"Yeah, I thought so. Check this out. It came back to England with a colonel. He reportedly bought it during the campaign." He hefts something that looks a bit like a tree stump and places it on his desk in front of you. "The man is supposed to have known Churchill."

"Which one?" You ask, but his face scrunches. Then your face scrunches. You can feel it. "What is it?"

"Look closely. He turned it ironically enough into a footstool."

You stare at the gray thing for a while until you understand. It's the foot of an elephant, hacked off and preserved somehow. Once you understand you lose yourself a little. All you can do is stare. "You have a lot of money, do you Drew?"

"What?"

"There is a point at which a man might have too much money." You realize that you're still at that age when so many things are injustices that you must rail against, and you like that about yourself, but it can be exhausting.

"What are you talking about?"

Cyndi and her mom come through the door on their quest to find you, and you turn to Drew, who is goggling at your wife and say, "Listen Drew, we're leaving now, and until you can find some way to act like a human being and get that stump out of here, we're not coming back."

"What?"

"Seriously, man, what the fuck is wrong with you?"

And as you walk out your daughter beams at you for the first time in a long time and it makes you want to storm out, which you do, as well as anyone can storm and also stop off by the bar for one more glass of the good stuff.

The King of Clap

Cyndi's been gone from the campfire for a while. Like any good parent, you check and find her behind a tent with Charley Miller's hand up under her shirt. He scampers off, but Cyndi folds her arms. "I thought you're supposed to be a liberal."

You raise your hands defensively. She's an adult now, and you've always talked about body autonomy. "I didn't say anything."

"Listen, Jerry Falwell, you're not going to tell me not to have sex."

"No, but have we had the birds and bees talk?"

"Yeah, once too often."

"One more time then. The Miller boy's a simpleton. My guess is that he's lugging around some virus. Maybe chlamydia."

Cyndi laughs. "Okay, tell me about the clap."

Autumn, winter, spring, it becomes a game. Halloween, you ask what her costume is, and she emails that she's going to be "The Miller boy's sexy sperm."

You write, "Send photos!!!"

At Christmas, she asks for *The Joy of Sex,* so you get her a Masters and Johnson library.

For her birthday, she asks you to take her to a Chippendales performance, and you do and throw in a calendar too.

The next summer around the fire, Cyndi whispers into your ear, "Charley's looking good."

"Remember me," you say, "as you're lying with him, and all the fun we've had this last year thinking about him."

"Jesus, Dad!" You've finally won your little game. She'll never look at the King of Clap in just the same way.

Mac and Cheese

For dinner tonight, you're having bourbon mac and cheese which is a little microwaved mac and cheese and a tall glass of bourbon as you watch reruns of *The Rockford Files* with the lights off on the old people channel. You've been having all your favorite meals while your wife's been off to her conference for this last week, bourbon French bread pizza, bourbon fish and chips, bourbon hamburger helper, all the hits.

Cyndi comes through the backdoor without knocking, without having called first, and flips on the light when you're about halfway through eating. She looks at your bounty and says, "Jesus, is that your dinner?"

"Only about half. The other half is inside me."

She looks at Jim Rockford who's about to be thrown into jail for the summer and says, "Do you know how dark this is?"

You sip your drink. "Only if you're conscious of what you're doing. Only if someone points it out."

"Mom said I should check in on you."

You look at yourself and your meal and think about your breakfast which was a similar sort of affair, beer pancakes. "I think she might have had a point, but on the other hand I've been watching *The Rockford Files* all day and thinking about a paper that I might write for a journal about white male aggression being fueled by a fear of a prison system that largely does not actually indict them for their crimes."

"Really?" She's trying to be angry, but you can see the humor slipping into her face.

"Truly. I have it about half-written." You tap your head with your index finger.

Now, she actually laughs. Her mother can work her up about stuff, and you can always calm her down. It's like dual superpowers that even each other out. "Come on. Sit down with me." She goes into the other room and brings a glass with her that she fills with some of your dinner. "Did I ever mansplain *The Rockford Files* to you?"

"Not yet."

"Would you like me to?"

"I'm worried about you."

"Now? I watched this show on reruns and drank when you were a baby. My behavior has maintained consistency. Ask any of my students then or now."

"Well, I guess I'm worried for you now and then too."

"Listen, Gumdrop, I'm not going to live forever. That much I know, but while I'm here I just want to hang out with you half-drunk and help you to understand mid-century sexism."

Cyndi groans, but she doesn't say anything. Instead she leans into you and you put your arm around her and think about her as a child. You think about the way you'd read to her and watch television with her, and you know that she thinks those words were insincere, but they were the truth. What you want now more than anything is time with her and her mother and these silly conversations that you have, so you point at the television and say, "That's a car we don't have any longer called a Pontiac Firebird."

Cyndi says, "No, slow down, you're going too fast for my feminine brain."

"I thought I might be," you say, and you hug her tight against you and remember what it was like to be young.

Eternal Return

You're in the room, part of the team helping your daughter Cyndi give birth, watching and cheering just as you watched and cheered when she was born, and you feel just as useless to the process now as you did then, maybe more so, but smart enough to keep your mouth shut on the subject both times. You're weeping as they hand your granddaughter to her, weeping and smiling. Later sitting next to her hospital bed you say, "You did it." You are here where Charles should be, but he's teaching and as far as you know, not aware that he's having a child today.

She's nursing her child, petting her head, and she says, "I love the little girl, but birth's no joke."

"Did you think it was going to be?"

"Lamaze doesn't prepare you."

"Well, at least you never have to go through that again," and wince on the inside hoping that she doesn't feel like this is you pointing fingers, questioning her choices.

She shrugs. "Not unless Nietzsche's concept of eternal return is correct, and I have to come back and do this over and over." She eyes you, she the school marm, and you the not so bright farm boy. "You know about eternal return, don't you?"

"Sure," you say. "Nietzsche and whatnot. You come back and do the same things forever. Always choosing the same things, always making the same mistakes."

She turns back to her daughter. "Did Charles teach you about that?"

"No, you did." And she did. You bought her master's thesis a year ago and read it four times before you felt that you fully understood it.

"I never used the word 'mistake.' That was all Charles."

"Yep, that's all Charles. He's the one who made all the mistakes. You're doing all right."

And at this moment, you hope Nietzsche is right about eternal return. You could come back to this here, and this now in the hospital watching your first grandchild come to know the world. It's worth dealing with Charles and his ponderous overblown speeches. It's worth your anger. It's worth every lousy moment with the asshole. You hope that Cyndi feels the same way too, and you think she does petting her daughter and beaming down on her. You think it's just like Charles to conflate fate with mistake. You think it's better through your lens than his.

Another Weirdo

Cyndi comes over to your place on a Tuesday after she bicycles your granddaughter off to school. Because you know she's coming, you have breakfast, bagels and bloody Marys waiting on the front porch. You're not sure what's in her bicycle basket, so you stare until you realize it's nine naked Barbie dolls, all decapitated.

"Are those yours or Tracie's?" you ask.

She gets off the bicycle and sits next to you on the wicker couch. "Kind of both. We made a deal. She gets to keep her decapitated women's army of the dead, but I hold on to them while she's in school."

"Seems fair."

"Her teacher wanted to make sure she didn't bring them to class any more. She thinks it's a little weird."

You look up into the sky. "Oh fuck her," you say. All your life, you've been dealing with adults who call children weird.

"You don't mind weird kids?"

"I don't think I'd like to meet a kid who wasn't weird. You were weird." You take a sip of your latest bloody Mary.

"Were you weird?"

"Sure."

"How?"

You think about it a moment and lift your glass. "I was a drunk."

That's not true but you were strange enough. Obsessed with bugs and pliers for some reason. You made your parents buy you a pair and then spent long hours trying to pull out nails or twist things.

"I certainly can believe that."

"It makes me tolerate all the weirdos in my life." You take another sip. "You want me to talk to this Nazi who's trying to indoctrinate my granddaughter."

Cyndi leans up against you. "No, not yet. If she makes Tracie wear matching socks, I'll give you a call, deal?"

"Deal." You hand her a glass of tomato juice. "Once again we have reached detente." And you clink glasses on it.

Can We Come out Now?

Somehow it occurs to you as Cyndi drives you past a mural of a dreamy panda on your way to the doctor that this is probably the last year of your life, that you've been spending more time with Cyndi than you have since she was in diapers, and you took that semester off to be a new dad, and that you hate the pandemic and all that it is doing, but that you are not going to come out now or ever again, and if that means that you can help Cyndi and she you, that's all right with you. You want this last year to be like your probably false memory of your first years, just you with a familial closeness that you've been craving your whole life since.

Balloons

Somehow it occurs to you as you pass the mural of the balloons nailed to the wall that if this is the last year of your life, that the memories that your daughter Cyndi has of you are fixed, solid. What you will be to her, you will always be and little that you do now will change that memory of you. There might be some touching moments. Maybe you'll have some rough arguments as the end of life emotions pop up here and there, but mostly what you have done is what you're going to be left with. You hope that she's left with the good memories mostly, not you making an ass of yourself, but little moments of hope like when the balloon slipped from her little hand and instead of crying, she pointed at it and held her breath it seemed for minutes until it got so far away it was no more, and she told you it was gone as though something leaving forever was a kind of miracle, and you suppose now that it was.

Bonobo

Somehow it occurs to you as you are passing the mural of the chimpanzee watching you calmly and quietly that his eyes are so much like your daughter Cyndi's eyes, especially when she was a child and would watch your every move so minutely. You thought then and you do now, that she could see into things in the way that others couldn't, but of course that might have just been a romanticization of childlike wisdom. Maybe it was right on however. You like to think it was because you thought then and you think now that she loved you deeply in those days, and if that were true then she both saw you deeply and still loved you despite your many deficiencies, and that is the most you can ask of anyone.

Time Will Heal

Somehow it occurs to you as Cyndi drives you to the doctor's appointment in what is almost certainly the last year of your life, that time does not heal everything, but that's perfectly fine with you. Looking back, you are grateful for what time has healed in you. It has healed the constant anxiety of your youth and the smug confidence of your middle years. It has healed you of worries over money and legacy. It has healed you of so many of your hatreds. It will not heal you from this last sickness eating away at your body, but perhaps it is not meant to. Perhaps, it's all right you think on a warm Inland Valley day in late September the light slanting in through the window across Cyndi's face, you warming into a nap and this moment when it's hard to remember if Cyndi is 49 or 16, you teaching her how to drive, you telling her not to worry so much, just to let go and allow the car to go where it is meant to go.

Pear

You're lying on the couch, pains shooting through you. Cyndi's in the next room making tea and cutting up a pear. You figure you have two months more to live if the doctors are right, and you're guessing they are.

This, it seems, is probably a moment for contemplation, and when you think back to childhood, you realize your best memory is that pear you had one day when you were four or five, the flavor more complex than any other fruit you'd ever had. Your dad handed it to you. You must have been on a trip because there was snow on the ground, but you lived in California.

Cyndi comes in and puts the plate with the cut up pear on the table next to you, and you say, "You know, I think my earliest memory was of a pear."

"Yeah," she says. "The one Grandpa gave you when you were a kid." She places the tea next to you too. "Why do you think I cut that up for you?"

You shake your head. "When did I tell you about that?" You thought you'd forgotten about it until just now.

She looks up at the popcorn ceiling. "I don't know. I was pretty little. You handed me a pear and told me about it. It's one of my favorite memories."

So all right, you think. That's it. That's the circle. The only thing left is to eat your fruit and let everything happen as it's going to happen. You must have worked through the other four stages, you suppose. So you pick up a slice and lift it to your nose. It smells of childhood and love. You bite into its complexity and think about nothing.

112 N. Harvard Ave. #65

Claremont, CA 91711

chapbooks@bamboodartpress.com

www.bamboodartpress.com